In 1935 if you wanted to
read a good book, you needed
either a lot of money or a library card.
Cheap paperbacks were available, but their
poor production generally mirrored the quality
between the covers. One weekend that year,
Allen Lane, Managing Director of The Bodley Head,
having spent the weekend visiting Agatha Christie,
found himself on a platform at Exeter station trying to
find something to read for his journey back to London.
He was appalled by the quality of the material he had to
choose from. Everything that Allen Lane achieved from that
day until his death in 1970 was based on a passionate belief
in the existence of 'a vast reading public for *intelligent*
books at a low price'. The result of his momentous vision
was the birth not only of Penguin, but of the 'paperback
revolution'. Quality writing became available for the price of
a packet of cigarettes, literature became a mass medium
for the first time, a nation of book-borrowers became a
nation of book-buyers – and the very concept of book
publishing was changed for ever. Those founding
principles – of quality and value, with an overarching
belief in the fundamental importance of reading –
have guided everything the company has
done since 1935. Sir Allen Lane's
pioneering spirit is still very much alive
at Penguin in 2005. Here's to
the next 70 years!

MORE THAN A BUSINESS

'We decided it was time to end the almost customary half-hearted manner in which cheap editions were produced – as though the only people who could possibly want cheap editions must belong to a lower order of intelligence. We, however, believed in the existence in this country of a vast reading public for intelligent books at a low price, and staked everything on it'
Sir Allen Lane, 1902–1970

'The Penguin Books are splendid value for sixpence, so splendid that if other publishers had any sense they would combine against them and suppress them'
George Orwell

'More than a business … a national cultural asset'
Guardian

'When you look at the whole Penguin achievement you know that it constitutes, in action, one of the more democratic successes of our recent social history'
Richard Hoggart

Innocent House

P. D. JAMES

PENGUIN BOOKS

PENGUIN BOOKS

Published by the Penguin Group
Penguin Books Ltd, 80 Strand, London WC2R ORL, England
Penguin Group (USA) Inc., 375 Hudson Street, New York, New York 10014, USA
Penguin Group (Canada), 10 Alcorn Avenue, Toronto, Ontario, Canada M4V 3B2
(a division of Pearson Penguin Canada Inc.)
Penguin Ireland, 25 St Stephen's Green, Dublin 2, Ireland
(a division of Penguin Books Ltd)
Penguin Group (Australia), 250 Camberwell Road, Camberwell, Victoria 3124,
Australia (a division of Pearson Australia Group Pty Ltd)
Penguin Books India Pvt Ltd, 11 Community Centre,
Panchsheel Park, New Delhi – 110 017, India
Penguin Group (NZ), cnr Airborne and Rosedale Roads, Albany,
Auckland 1310, New Zealand (a division of Pearson New Zealand Ltd)
Penguin Books (South Africa) (Pty) Ltd, 24 Sturdee Avenue,
Rosebank 2196, South Africa

Penguin Books Ltd, Registered Offices: 80 Strand, London WC2R ORL, England

www.penguin.com

Original Sin first published by Faber & Faber 1994
First published in Penguin Books 1995
This extract published as a Pocket Penguin 2005

2

Copyright © P. D. James, 1994
All rights reserved

The moral right of the author has been asserted

Set in 11/13pt Monotype Dante
Typeset by Palimpsest Book Production Limited
Polmont, Stirlingshire
Printed in England by Clays Ltd, St Ives plc

For a temporary shorthand-typist to be present at the discovery of a corpse on the first day of a new assignment, if not unique, is sufficiently rare to prevent its being regarded as an occupational hazard. Certainly Mandy Price, aged nineteen years two months, and the acknowledged star of Mrs Crealey's Nonesuch Secretarial Agency, set out on the morning of Tuesday, 14 September for her interview at the Peverell Press with no more apprehension than she usually felt at the start of a new job, an apprehension which was never acute and was rooted less in any anxiety whether she would satisfy the expectations of the prospective employer than in whether the employer would satisfy hers. She had learned of the job the previous Friday when she called in at the agency at six o'clock to collect her pay after a boring two-week stint with a director who regarded a secretary as a status symbol but had no idea how to use her skills, and she was ready for something new and preferably exciting although perhaps not as exciting as it was subsequently to prove.

Mrs Crealey, for whom Mandy had worked for the past three years, conducted her agency from a couple of rooms above a newsagent and tobacconist's shop off the Whitechapel Road, a situation which, she was fond of pointing out to her girls and clients, was convenient both for the City and for the towering offices of Docklands. Neither had so far produced much in the way of business, but while other agencies foundered in the waves of recession Mrs Crealey's small and underprovisioned ship was still, if precariously, afloat. Except for the help of one of her girls when no outside work was available, she ran the agency single-handed. The outer room was her office in which she propitiated clients, interviewed new girls and assigned the next week's work. The inner was her personal sanctum, furnished with a divan bed on which she occasionally spent the night in defiance of the terms of the lease, a drinks cabinet and refrigerator, a cupboard which opened to reveal a minute kitchen, a large television set and two easy chairs set in front of a gas fire in which a lurid red light rotated behind artificial logs. She referred to her room as the 'cosy', and Mandy was one of the few girls who were admitted to its privacies.

It was probably the cosy which kept Mandy faithful to the agency, although she would never have openly admitted to a need which would have seemed to her both childish and embarrassing. Her mother had left home when she was six and she herself had been hardly able to wait for her sixteenth birthday when she could get away from a father whose idea of parenthood had gone little further than the provision of two meals a day, which she was expected to cook, and her clothes. For the last year she had rented one room in a terraced house in Stratford East where she lived in acrimonious camaraderie with three young friends, the main cause of dispute being Mandy's insistence that her Yamaha motor bike should be parked in the narrow hall. But it was the cosy in Whitechapel Road, the mingled smells of wine and takeaway Chinese food, the hiss of the gas fire, the two deep and battered armchairs in which she could curl up and sleep which represented all Mandy had ever known of the comfort and security of a home.

Mrs Crealey, sherry bottle in one hand and a scrap of jotting pad in the other, munched at her cigarette holder until she had manoeuvred it to the corner of her mouth where, as usual, it hung in defiance of gravity, and squinted at her almost indecipherable hand-writing through immense horn-rimmed spectacles.

'It's a new client, Mandy, the Peverell Press. I've looked them up in the publishers' directory. They're one of the oldest – perhaps the oldest – publishing firms in the country, founded in 1792. Their place is on the river. The Peverell Press, Innocent House, Innocent Walk, Wapping. You must have seen Innocent House if you've taken a boat trip to Greenwich. Looks like a bloody great Venetian palace. They do have a launch, apparently, to collect staff from Charing Cross pier, but that'll be no help to you, living in Stratford. It's your side of the Thames, though, which will help with the journey. I suppose you'd better take a taxi. Mind you get them to pay before you leave.'

'That's OK, I'll use the bike.'

'Just as you like. They want you there on Tuesday at ten o'clock.'

Mrs Crealey was about to suggest that, with this prestigious new client, a certain formality of dress might be appropriate, but desisted. Mandy was amenable to some suggestions about work or behaviour but never about the eccentric and occasionally bizarre creations with which she expressed her essentially confident and ebullient personality.

She asked: 'Why Tuesday? Don't they work Mondays?'

'Don't ask me. All I know is that the girl who rang said Tuesday. Perhaps Miss Etienne can't see you until then. She's one of the directors and she wants to interview you personally. Miss Claudia Etienne. I've written it all down.'

Mandy said: 'What's the big deal then? Why have I got to be interviewed by the boss?'

'One of the bosses. They're particular who they get, I suppose. They asked for the best and I'm sending the best. Of course they may be looking for someone permanent, and want to try her out first. Don't let them persuade you to stay on, Mandy, will you?'

'Have I ever?'

Accepting a glass of sweet sherry and curling into one of the easy chairs, Mandy studied the paper. It was certainly odd to be interviewed by a prospective employer before beginning a new job even when, as now, the client was new to the agency. The usual procedure was well understood by all parties. The harassed employer telephoned Mrs Crealey for a temporary shorthand-typist, imploring her this time to send a girl who was literate and whose typing speed at least approximated to the standard claimed. Mrs Crealey, promising miracles of punctuality, efficiency and conscientiousness, dispatched whichever of her girls was free and could be cajoled into giving the job a try, hoping that this time the expectations of client and worker might actually coincide. Subsequent complaints were countered by Mrs Crealey's invariably plaintive response: 'I can't understand it. She's got the highest reports from other employers. I'm always being asked for Sharon.'

The client, made to feel that the disaster was somehow his or her fault, replaced the receiver with a sigh, urged, encouraged, endured until the mutual agony was over and the permanent member of staff returned to a flattering welcome. Mrs Crealey took her commission, more modest than was charged by most agencies, which probably accounted for her continued existence in business, and the transaction was over until the next epidemic of flu or the summer holidays provoked another triumph of hope over experience.

Mrs Crealey said: 'You can take Monday off, Mandy, on full pay of course. And better type out your qualifications and experience. Put "Curriculum Vitae" at the top, that always looks impressive.'

Mandy's curriculum vitae, and Mandy herself – despite her eccentric appearance – never failed to impress. For this she had to thank her English teacher, Mrs Chilcroft. Mrs Chilcroft, facing her class of recalcitrant eleven-year-olds, had said: 'You are going to learn to write your own language simply, accurately and with some elegance, and to speak it so that you aren't disadvantaged the moment you open your mouths. If any of you has ambitions above marrying at sixteen and rearing children in a council flat you'll need language. If you've no ambitions beyond being supported by a man or the State you'll need it even more, if only to get the better of the local authority Social Services department and the DSS. But learn it you will.'

Mandy could never decide whether she hated or admired Mrs Chilcroft, but under her inspired if unconventional teaching she had learned to speak English, to write, to spell and to use it confidently and with some grace. Most of the time this was an accomplishment she preferred to pretend she hadn't achieved. She thought, although she never articulated the heresy, that there was little point in being at home in Mrs Chilcroft's world if she ceased to be accepted in her own. Her literacy was there to be used when necessary, a commercial and occasionally a social asset, to which Mandy added high shorthand-typing speeds and a facility with various types of word processor. Mandy knew herself to be highly employable, but remained faithful to Mrs Crealey. Apart from the cosy there were obvious advantages in being regarded as indispensable; one could be sure of getting the pick of the jobs. Her male employers occasionally tried to persuade her to take a permanent post, some of them offering inducements which had little to do with annual increments, luncheon vouchers or generous pension contributions. Mandy remained with the Nonesuch Agency, her fidelity rooted in more than material considerations. She occasionally felt for her employer an almost adult compassion. Mrs Crealey's troubles principally arose from her conviction of the perfidy of men combined with an inability to do without them. Apart from this uncomfortable dichotomy, her life was dominated by a fight to retain the few girls in her stable who were employable, and her war of attrition against her ex-husband, the tax inspector, her bank manager and her office landlord. In all these traumas Mandy was ally, confidante and sympathizer. Where Mrs Crealey's love-life was concerned this was more from an easy goodwill than from any understanding, since to Mandy's nineteen-year-old mind the possibility that her employer could actually wish to have sex with the elderly – some of them must be at least fifty – and unprepossessing males who occasionally haunted the office, was too bizarre to warrant serious contemplation.

After a week of almost continuous rain Tuesday promised to be a fine day with gleams of fitful sunshine shafting through the low clusters of cloud.

The ride from Stratford East wasn't long, but Mandy left plenty of time and it was only a quarter to ten when she turned off The Highway, down Garnet Street and along Wapping Wall, then right into Innocent Walk. Reducing speed to a walking pace, she bumped along a wide cobbled cul-de-sac bounded on the north by a ten-foot wall of grey brick and on the south by the three houses which comprised the Peverell Press.

At first sight she thought Innocent House disappointing. It was an imposing but unremarkable Georgian house with proportions which she knew rather than felt to be graceful, and it looked little different from the many others she had seen in London's squares or terraces. The front door was closed and she saw no sign of activity behind the four storeys of eight-paned windows, the two lowest ones each with an elegant wrought-iron balcony. On either side was a smaller, less ostentatious house, standing a little distanced and detached like a pair of deferential poor relations. She was now opposite the first of these, number 10, although she could see no sign of numbers 1 to 9, and saw that it was separated from the main building by Innocent Passage, barred from the road by a wrought-iron gate, and obviously used as a parking space for staff cars. But now the gate was open and Mandy saw three men bringing down large cardboard cartons by a hoist from an upper floor and loading them into a small van. One of the three, a swarthy under-sized man wearing a battered bush-ranger's hat, took it off and swept Mandy a low ironic bow. The other two glanced up from their work to regard her with obvious curiosity. Mandy, pushing up her visor, bestowed on all three of them a long discouraging stare.

The second of these smaller houses was separated from Innocent House by Innocent Lane. It was here, according to Mrs Crealey's instructions, that she would find the entrance. She switched off the engine, dismounted, and wheeled the bike over the cobbles, looking for the most unobtrusive place in which to park. It was then that she had her first glimpse of the river, a narrow glitter of shivering water under the lightening sky. Parking the Yamaha, she took off her crash helmet, rummaged for her hat in the side pannier and put it on, and then, with the helmet under her arm, and carrying her tote bag, she walked towards the water as if physically drawn by the strong tug of the tide, the faint evocative sea smell.

She found herself on a wide forecourt of gleaming marble bounded by a low railing in delicate wrought iron with at each corner a glass globe supported by entwined dolphins in bronze. From a gap in the middle of the railing a flight of steps led down to the river. She could hear its rhythmic slap against the stone. She walked slowly towards it in a trance of wonder as if she had never seen it before. It shimmered before her, a wide expanse of heaving sun-speckled water which, as she watched, was flicked by the strengthening breeze into a million small waves like a restless inland sea, and then, as the breeze dropped, mysteriously subsided into shining smoothness. And, turning, she saw for the first time the towering wonder of Innocent House, four storeys of coloured marble and golden stone which, as the light changed, seemed subtly to change colour, brightening, then shading to a deeper gold. The great curved arch of the main entrance was flanked by narrow arched windows and above it were two storeys with wide balconies of carved stone fronting a row of slender marble pillars rising to trefoiled arches. The high arched windows and marble columns extended to a final storey under the parapet of a low roof. She knew none of the architectural details but she had seen houses like this before, on a boisterous ill-conducted school trip to Venice when she was thirteen. The city had left little impression on her beyond the high summer reek of the canal, which had caused the children to hold their noses and scream in simulated disgust, the over-crowded picture galleries and palaces which she was told were remarkable but which looked as if they were about to crumble into the canals. She had seen Venice when she was too young and inadequately prepared. Now for the first time in her life, looking up at the marvel of Innocent House, she felt a belated response to that earlier experience, a mixture of awe and joy which surprised and a little frightened her.

The trance was broken by a male voice: 'Looking for someone?'

Turning, she saw a man looking at her through the railings, as if he had risen miraculously from the river. Walking over, she saw that he was standing in the bow of a launch moored to the left of the steps. He was wearing a yachting cap set well back on a mop of black curls and his eyes were bright slits in the weatherbeaten face.

She said: 'I've come about a job. I was just looking at the river.'

'Oh, she's always here is the river. The entrance is down there.' He cocked a thumb towards Innocent Lane.

'Yes, I know.'

To demonstrate independence of action, Mandy glanced at her watch, then turned and spent another two minutes regarding Innocent House. With a final glance at the river she made her way down Innocent Lane.

The outer door bore a notice: PEVERELL PRESS – PLEASE ENTER. She pushed it open and passed through a glass vestibule and into the reception office. To the left was a curved desk and a switchboard manned by a grey-haired, gentle-faced man who greeted her with a smile before checking her name on a list. Mandy handed him her crash helmet and he received it into his small age-speckled hands as carefully as if it were a bomb, and for a few moments seemed uncertain what to do with it, finally leaving it on the counter.

He announced her arrival by telephone, then said:

'Miss Blackett will come to take you up to Miss Etienne. Perhaps you would like to take a seat.'

Mandy sat and, ignoring the three daily newspapers, the literary magazines and the carefully arranged catalogues fanned out on a low table, looked about her. It must once have been an elegant room; the marble fireplace with an oil painting of the Grand Canal set in the panel above it, the delicate stuccoed ceiling and the carved cornice contrasted incongruously with the modern reception desk, the comfortable but utilitarian chairs, the large baize-covered noticeboard and the caged lift to the right of the fireplace. The walls painted a dark rich green bore a row of sepia portraits. Mandy supposed they were of previous Peverells and had just got to her feet to have a closer look when her escort appeared, a sturdy, rather plain woman who was presumably Miss Blackett. She greeted Mandy unsmilingly, cast a surprised and rather startled look at her hat and, without introducing herself, invited Mandy to follow her. Mandy was unworried by her lack of warmth. This was obviously the managing director's PA, anxious to demonstrate her status. Mandy had met her kind before.

The hall made her gasp with wonder. She saw a floor of patterned marble in coloured segments from which six slim pillars rose with intricately carved capitals to an amazing painted ceiling. Ignoring Miss Blackett's obvious impatience as she lingered on the bottom step of the staircase, Mandy unselfconsciously paused and slowly turned, eyes upwards, while above her the great coloured dome spun slowly with her; palaces, towers with their floating banners, churches, houses, bridges, the curving river plumed with the sails of high-masted ships and small cherubs with pouted lips blowing prosperous breezes in small bursts like steam from a kettle. Mandy had worked in a variety of offices, from glass towers furnished with chrome and leather and the latest electronic wonders to rooms as small as cupboards with one wooden table and an ancient typewriter, and had early learned that the office ambience was an unreliable guide to the firm's financial standing. But never before had she seen an office building like Innocent House.

They mounted the wide double staircase without speaking. Miss Etienne's office was on the first floor. It had obviously once been a library but the end had been partitioned to provide a small office. A serious-faced young woman, so thin she looked anorexic, was typing on a word processor and gave Mandy only a brief glance. Miss Blackett opened the interconnecting door and announced: 'It's Mandy Price from the agency, Miss Claudia,' then left.

The room seemed to Mandy very large after the ill-proportioned outer office and she walked across an expanse of parquet flooring towards a desk set to the right of the far window. A tall dark woman got up to receive her, shook hands and motioned her to the opposite chair.

She said: 'You have your curriculum vitae?'

'Yes, Miss Etienne.'

Never before had she been asked for a CV, but Mrs Crealey had been right; obviously one was expected. Mandy reached down to her tasselled and garishly embroidered tote bag, a trophy from last summer's holiday in Crete, and handed over three carefully typed pages. Miss Etienne studied them and Mandy studied Miss Etienne.

She decided that she wasn't young, certainly over thirty. Her face was sharp-boned with a pale delicate skin, the eyes shallowly set with dark, almost black, irises under heavy lids. Above them the brows had been plucked to a high arch. The short hair, brushed to a sheen, was parted on the left side, the falling strands tucked behind her right ear. The hands which rested on the CV were ringless, the fingers very long and slender, the nails unpainted.

Without looking up, she asked: 'Is your name Mandy or Amanda Price?'

'Mandy, Miss Etienne.' In other circumstances Mandy would have pointed out that if her name were Amanda the CV would have said so.

'Have you had any previous experience of working in a publishing house?'

'Only about three times during the last two years. I've listed the names of the firms I've worked for on page three of my CV.'

Miss Etienne read on, then looked up, the bright luminous eyes under the curved brows studying Mandy with more interest than she had previously shown.

She said: 'You seem to have done very well at school, but you've had an extraordinary variety of jobs since. You haven't stuck to any of them for more than a few weeks.'

In three years of temping Mandy had learned to recognize and circumvent most of the machinations of the male sex, but was less assured when it came to dealing with her own. Her instinct, sharp as a ferret's tooth, told her that Miss Etienne might need careful handling. She thought, that's what being a temp is, you silly old cow. Here today and gone tomorrow. What she said was: 'That's why I like temporary work. I want to get as wide a variety of experience as possible before I settle down to a permanent job. Once I do, I'd like to stay on and try to make a success of it.'

Mandy was being less than candid. She had no intention of taking a permanent job. Temporary work, with its freedom from contracts and conditions of service, its variety, the knowledge that she wasn't tied down, that even the worst job experience could end by the following Friday, suited her perfectly; her plans, however, lay elsewhere. Mandy was saving for the day when, with her friend Naomi, she could afford a small lock-up shop in the Portobello Road. There Naomi would fashion her jewellery and Mandy would design and make her hats, both of them rising rapidly to fame and fortune.

Miss Etienne looked again at the curriculum vitae. She said drily: 'If your ambition is to find a permanent job then make a success of it, you are certainly unique in your generation.'

She handed back the curriculum vitae with a quick impatient gesture, rose to her feet, and said: 'All right, we'll give you a typing test. Let's see if you're as good as you claim. There's a second word processor in Miss Blackett's office on the ground floor. That's where you'll be working so you may as well do the test there. Mr Dauntsey, our poetry editor, has a tape he wants transcribed. It's in the little archives office.' She got up and added, 'We'll fetch it together. You may as well get some idea of the layout of the house.'

Mandy said: 'Poetry?' This could be tricky, typing from tape. From her experience it was difficult with modern verse to know where the lines began and ended.

'Not poetry. Mr Dauntsey is examining and reporting on the archives, recommending which files should be retained, which destroyed. The Peverell Press has been publishing since 1792. There's some interesting material in the old files and it ought to be properly catalogued.'

Mandy followed Miss Etienne down the wide curved stairs, across the hall and into the reception room. Apparently they were to use the lift and it ran only from the ground floor. It was hardly, she thought, the best way to get an idea of the layout of the house, but the comment had been promising; it looked as if the job was hers if she wanted it. And from that first view of the Thames, Mandy knew that she did want it.

The lift was small, little more than five feet square, and as they groaned upwards she was sharply aware of the tall silent figure whose arm almost brushed her own. She kept her eyes fixed on the grid of the lift but she could smell Miss Etienne's scent, subtle and a little exotic but so faint that perhaps it wasn't scent at all but only an expensive soap. Everything about Miss Etienne seemed to Mandy expensive, the dull sheen of the shirt which could only be silk, the double gold chain and gold stud earrings, the cardigan casually slung around her shoulders which had the fine softness of cashmere. But the physical closeness of her companion and her own heightened senses, stimulated by the novelty and excitement of Innocent House, told her something more; that Miss Etienne wasn't at ease. It was she, Mandy, who should have been nervous. Instead she was aware that the air of the claustrophobic lift, jerking upwards with such maddening slowness, was quivering with tension.

They shuddered to a stop and Miss Etienne hauled back the double-grille gates. Mandy found herself in a narrow hall with a facing door and one on the left. The door ahead was open and she saw a large cluttered room filled from floor to ceiling with metal shelves tightly packed with files and bundles of papers. The racks ran from the windows to the door with just enough room to walk between them. The air smelt of old paper, musty and stale. She followed Miss Etienne between the ends of the shelves and the wall and to another smaller door, this time closed.

Pausing, Miss Etienne said: 'Mr Dauntsey works on the files in here. We call it the little archives office. He said that he'd leave the tape on the table.'

It seemed to Mandy that the explanation was unnecessary and rather odd, and that Miss Etienne hesitated for a second, hand on the knob, before turning it. Then with a sharp gesture, almost as if she expected some obstruction, she pushed the door wide open.

The stink rolled out to meet them like an evil wraith, the familiar human smell of vomit, not strong but so unexpected that Mandy instinctively recoiled. Over Miss Etienne's shoulder her eyes took in at once a small room with an uncarpeted wooden floor, a square table to the right of the door and a single high window. Under the window was a narrow divan bed and on the bed sprawled a woman.

It had needed no smell to tell Mandy that she was looking at death. She didn't scream; she had never screamed from fear or shock; but a giant fist mailed in ice clutched and squeezed her heart and stomach and she began shivering as violently as a child lifted from an icy sea. Neither of them spoke but, with Mandy close behind Miss Etienne, they moved with quiet almost imperceptible steps closer to the bed.

She was lying on top of a tartan rug but had taken the single pillow from beneath it to rest her head as if needing this final comfort even in the last moments of consciousness. By the bed stood a chair holding an empty wine bottle, a stained tumbler and a large screw-top jar. Beneath it a pair of brown laced shoes had been neatly laid side by side. Perhaps, thought Mandy, she had taken them off because she hadn't wanted to soil the rug. But the rug was soiled and so was the pillow. There was a slime of vomit like the track of a giant snail gummed to the left cheek and stiffening the pillow. The woman's eyes were half open, the irises turned upward, her grey hair, worn in a fringe, was hardly disarranged. She was wearing a brown high-necked jumper and a tweed skirt from which two skinny legs, oddly twisted, stuck out like sticks. Her left arm was flung outwards, almost touching the chair, the right lay across her breast. The right hand had scrabbled at the thin wool of the jumper before death, drawing it up to reveal a few inches of white vest. Beside the empty pill bottle there was a square envelope addressed in strong black handwriting.

Mandy whispered as reverently as if she were in church: 'Who is she?'

Miss Etienne's voice was calm. 'Sonia Clements. One of our senior editors.'

'Was I going to work for her?'

Mandy knew the question was irrelevant as soon as she asked it, but Miss Etienne replied: 'For part of the time, yes, but not for long. She was leaving at the end of the month.'

She picked up the envelope, seeming to weigh it in her hands. Mandy thought, she wants to open it but not in front of me. After a few seconds Miss Etienne said: 'Addressed to the coroner. It's obvious enough what's happened here even without this. I'm sorry you've had this shock, Miss Price. It was inconsiderate of her. If people wish to kill themselves they should do so in their own homes.'

Mandy thought of the small terrace in Stratford East, the shared kitchen and one bathroom, her own small back room in a house in which you'd be lucky to find enough privacy to swallow the pills, let alone die of them. She made herself gaze again at the woman's face. She felt a sudden urge to close the eyes and shut the slightly gaping mouth. So this was death, or rather this was death before the undertakers got their hands on you. Mandy had seen only one other dead person, her gran; neatly shrouded with a frill at her neck, packaged into her coffin like a doll in a gift box, curiously diminished and looking more peaceful than Gran ever had in life, the bright restless eyes closed, the over-busy hands folded in quietude at last. Suddenly grief came upon her in a torrent of pity, perhaps released by delayed shock or the sudden acute memory of the gran whom she had loved. At the first hot prick of tears she wasn't sure whether they were for Gran or for this stranger sprawled in such defenceless ungainliness. She seldom cried but when she did her tears were unstoppable. Terrified she would disgrace herself she fought for control and, gazing round, her eyes lit on something familiar, unfrightening, something she could cope with, an assurance that there was an ordinary world continuing outside this death-cell. On the table was a small tape recorder.

Mandy went over to it and closed her hand round it as if it were an icon. She said, 'Is this the tape? Is it a list? Do you want it tabulated?'

Miss Etienne regarded her for a moment in silence, then she said, 'Yes, tabulate it. And two copies. You can use the word processor in Miss Blackett's office.'

And in that moment Mandy knew that she had the job.

2

Fifteen minutes earlier Gerard Etienne, chairman and managing director of Peverell Press, was leaving the boardroom to return to his office on the ground floor. Suddenly he stopped, stepped back into the shadows, delicate-footed as a cat, and stood watching from behind the balustrade. Below him in the hall a girl was slowly pirouetting, her eyes upward to the ceiling. She was wearing thigh-length black boots flared at the top, a short tight fawn skirt and a velvet jacket in a dull red. One thin and delicate arm was raised to hold on her head a remarkable hat. It seemed to be made of red felt and was wide-brimmed, turned up at the front and decorated with an extraordinary array of objects: flowers, feathers, strips of satin and lace, even small fragments of glass. As she turned it flashed and gleamed and glittered. She should, he thought, have looked ridiculous, the peaked childish face half-hidden by untidy swathes of dark hair, topped by such a grotesque confection. Instead she looked enchanting. He found himself smiling, almost laughing, and was suddenly seized with a madness he hadn't felt since he was twenty-one, the urge to rush down the wide staircase, sweep her into his arms and dance with her across the marble floor, out through the front door and to the rim of the glittering river. She had finished her slow turn and followed Miss Blackett across the hall. He stood for a moment savouring this upsurge of folly which, it seemed to him, had nothing to do with sex but the need to hold distilled a memory of youth, of early loves, of laughter, of freedom from responsibility, of sheer animal delight in the world of the senses. None of it had any part in his life now. He was still smiling as he waited until the hall was clear and then slowly descended to his office.

Twenty minutes later the door opened and he recognized his sister's footsteps. Without looking up he said: 'Who is the child in the hat?'

'The hat?' For a moment she seemed not to understand, then she said: 'Oh, the hat. Mandy Price from the secretarial agency.'

There was an odd note in her voice and he turned, giving her his full attention. He said, 'Claudia, what's happened?'

'Sonia Clements is dead. Suicide.'

'Where?'

'Here. In the little archives office. The girl and I found her. We were fetching one of Gabriel's tapes.'

'That girl found her?' He paused and added, 'Where is she now?'

'I've told you, in the little archives office. We didn't touch the body. Why should we?'

'I mean where is the child?'

'Next door with Blackie working on the tape. Don't

waste your pity. She wasn't alone and there isn't any blood. That generation is tough. She didn't blink an eye. All she worried about was getting the job.'

'You're sure it was suicide?'

'Of course. She left this note. It's open but I haven't read it.'

She handed over the envelope then walked to the window and stood looking out. After a couple of seconds he slid out the flap and drew the paper carefully from the envelope, then read aloud. '"I am sorry to cause a nuisance but this seemed the best room to use. Gabriel will probably be the one to find me and he's too familiar with death to be shocked. Now that I live alone I might not have been discovered at home until I began to stink and I find that one has the need to preserve some dignity, even in death. My affairs are in order, and I have written to my sister. I am under no obligation to give a reason for my act, but in case anyone is interested it is simply that I prefer annihilation to continued existence. It is a reasonable choice and one which we are all entitled to make."'

He said: 'Well that's clear enough, and in her own hand. How did she do it?'

'With drugs and drink. There isn't much mess, as I said.'

'Have you phoned the police?'

'The police? I haven't had time yet. I came straight to you. And is it really necessary, Gerard? Suicide isn't a crime. Can't we just ring Dr Frobisher?'

He said curtly, 'I don't know whether it's necessary but it's certainly expedient. We don't want any doubts about this death.'

'Doubts?' she said. 'Doubts? Why should there be doubts?'

She had lowered her voice and now they were almost whispering. Almost imperceptibly they moved further from the partition towards the window.

He said: 'Gossip then, rumours, scandal. We can phone the police from here. There's no point in going through the switchboard. If they bring her down in the lift we can probably get her out of the building before the staff know what's happened. There's George of course. I suppose that the police had better come in by that door. George will have to be told to keep his mouth shut. Where is the agency girl now?'

'I've told you. Next door in Blackie's room, doing her typing test.'

'Or, more likely, describing to Blackie and anyone else who comes by how she was taken upstairs to get a tape and found a dead body.'

'I've instructed them both to say nothing until we've told all the staff. Gerard, if you think you can keep this quiet even for a couple of hours, forget it. There'll be an inquest, publicity. And they'll have to bring her down by the stairs. You can't possibly fit a body bag on a stretcher in the lift. My God, though, this is all we needed! Coming on top of the other business it's going to be great for staff morale.'

There was a moment's silence in which neither

moved towards the telephone. Then she looked at him and asked: 'When you sacked her last Wednesday, how did she take it?'

'She didn't kill herself because I gave her the push. She was a rational woman, she knew she had to go. She must have known that from the day I took over here. I always made it clear that I thought we had one editor too many, that we could farm out the work to a freelance.'

'But she's fifty-three. It wouldn't have been easy for her to get another job. And she's been here for twenty-four years.'

'Part-time.'

'Part-time but working almost full-time. This place was her life.'

'Claudia, that's sentimental nonsense. She had an existence outside these walls. What the hell has that to do with it anyway? Either she was needed here or she wasn't.'

'And is that how you broke it to her? No longer needed.'

'I wasn't brutal, if that's what you're implying. I told her that I proposed to employ a freelance for some of the non-fiction editing and that her post was therefore superfluous. I said that although she didn't legally qualify for maximum redundancy pay we would come to some financial arrangement.'

'Arrangement? What did she say?'

'She said that it wouldn't be necessary. She would make her own arrangements.'

'And she has. Apparently with distalgesic and a bottle of Bulgarian cabernet. Well at least she's saved us money but, by God, I'd rather have paid out than be faced with this. I know I ought to feel pity for her. I suppose I shall when I've got over the shock. Just now it isn't easy.'

'Claudia, it's pointless to reopen all those old arguments. It was necessary to sack her and I sacked her. That had nothing to do with her death. I did what had to be done in the interests of the firm and at the time you agreed. Neither you nor I can be blamed for her suicide and her death has nothing to do with the other mischief here either.' He paused then said: 'Unless of course she was the one responsible.'

She didn't miss the sudden note of hope in his voice. So he was more worried than he would admit. She said bitterly: 'That would be a neat way out of our troubles, wouldn't it? But how could she have been, Gerard? She was off sick, remember, when the Stilgoe proofs were tampered with and visiting an author in Brighton when we lost the illustrations for the Guy Fawkes book. No, she's in the clear.'

'Of course. Yes, I'd forgotten. Look, I'll ring the police now while you go round the office and explain what's happened. That's less dramatic than getting everyone together for a general announcement. Tell them to stay in their rooms until the body has been removed.'

She said slowly: 'There is one thing. I think I was the last person to see her alive.'

'Someone had to be.'

'It was last night, just after seven. I was working late. I came out of the cloakroom on the first floor and saw her going up the stairs. She was carrying a bottle of wine and a glass.'

'You didn't ask her what she was doing?'

'Of course I didn't. She wasn't a junior typist. For all I knew she was taking the wine to the archives room to do a spot of secret drinking. If so it was hardly my concern. I thought it odd that she was working so late, but that's all.'

'Did she see you?'

'I don't think so. She didn't look round.'

'And no one else was about?'

'Not at that hour. I was the last.'

'Then say nothing about it. It isn't relevant. It doesn't help.'

'I did have a feeling, though, that there was something strange about her. She did look – well – furtive. She was almost scurrying.'

'That's hindsight. You didn't check on the building before you locked up?'

'I looked in her room. The light wasn't on. There was nothing there, no coat, no bag. I suppose she'd locked them in her cupboard. Obviously I thought she'd left and gone home.'

'You can say that at the inquest, but no more. Don't mention seeing her earlier. It might only lead the coroner to ask why you didn't check the top of the building.'

'Why should I?'

'Exactly.'

'But Gerard, if I'm asked when I saw her last . . .'

'Then lie. But for God's sake, Claudia, lie convincingly and stick with the lie.' He moved over to the desk and lifted the receiver. 'I suppose I'd better dial 999. It's odd, but this is the first time in my memory that we've ever had the police at Innocent House.'

She turned from the window and looked full at him. 'Let's hope that it's the last.'

3

In the outer office Mandy and Miss Blackett sat each at her word processor, each typing, eyes fixed on the screen. Neither spoke. At first Mandy's fingers had refused to work, trembling uncertainly over the keys as if the letters had been inexplicably transposed and the whole keyboard had become a meaningless jumble of symbols. But she clasped her hands tightly in her lap for half a minute and by an effort of will brought the shaking under control, and when she actually began typing the familiar skill took over and all was well. From time to time she glanced quickly at Miss Blackett. The woman was obviously deeply shocked. The large face with its marsupial cheeks and small, rather obstinate mouth was so white that Mandy feared that at any moment she would slump forward over the keyboard in a faint.

It was over half an hour since Miss Etienne and her brother had left. Within ten minutes of closing the door Miss Etienne had put her head round it and had said: 'I've asked Mrs Demery to bring you some tea. It's been a shock for both of you.'

The tea had come within minutes, carried in by a red-haired woman in a flowered apron who had put down the tray on top of a filing cabinet with the words: 'I'm not supposed to talk so I won't. No harm in telling you, though, that the police have just arrived. That's quick work. No doubt they'll be wanting tea now.' She had then disappeared, as if aware that there was more excitement to be had outside the room than in.

Miss Blackett's office was an ill-proportioned room, too narrow for its height, the discordancy emphasized by the splendid marble fireplace with its formal patterned frieze, the heavy mantelshelf supported by the heads of two sphinxes. The partition, wooden for the bottom three feet with paned glass above, cut across one of the narrow arched windows as well as bisecting a lozenge-shaped decoration on the ceiling. Mandy thought that if the large room had had to be divided, it could have been done with more sensitivity to the architecture, not to mention Miss Blackett's convenience. This way it gave the impression that she was grudged even enough space in which to work.

Another but different oddity was the long snake in striped green velvet curled between the handles of the two top drawers of the steel filing cabinets. Its bright button eyes were crowned with a minute top hat and its forked tongue in red flannel hung from a soft open mouth lined with what looked like pink silk. Mandy had seen similar snakes before; her gran had had one. They were intended to be laid along the bottom of doors to exclude draughts, or wound round the handles to keep the door ajar. But it was a ridiculous object, a kind of kid's toy, and hardly one she had expected to see in Innocent House. She would have liked to have asked Miss Blackett about it but Miss Etienne had told them not to talk and Miss Blackett was obviously interpreting this as prohibiting all speech except about work.

The minutes passed silently. Mandy would shortly be at the end of her tape. Then Miss Blackett, looking up, said: 'You can stop that now. I'll give you some dictation. Miss Etienne wanted me to test your shorthand.'

She took one of the firm's catalogues from her desk drawer, handed Mandy a notebook, moved her chair beside her and began reading in a low voice, hardly moving her almost bloodless lips. Mandy's fingers automatically formed the familiar hieroglyphics but her mind took in few of the details of the forthcoming non-fiction list. From time to time Miss Blackett's voice faltered and Mandy knew that she too was listening to the sounds outside. After the initial sinister silence, they could now hear footsteps, half-imagined whispering, and then louder footfalls echoing on the marble and confident masculine voices.

Miss Blackett, her eyes on the door, said tonelessly: 'Perhaps you'd read it back now?'

Mandy read back her shorthand faultlessly. Again there was a silence. Then the door opened and Miss Etienne came in. She said: 'The police have arrived. They are just waiting for the police surgeon and then they'll be taking Miss Clements away. You'd better stay here until it's all clear.' She looked at Miss Blackett. 'Have you finished the test?'

'Yes, Miss Claudia.'

Mandy handed up her typed lists. Miss Etienne glanced at them dismissively and said: 'Right, the job is yours if you want it. Start tomorrow at nine-thirty.'

4

Ten days after Sonia Clements' suicide and exactly three weeks before the first of the Innocent House murders, Adam Dalgliesh lunched with Conrad Ackroyd at the Cadaver Club. It was at Ackroyd's invitation, given by telephone with that conspiratorial and slightly portentous air with which all Conrad's invitations were invested. Even a duty dinner party given to pay off outstanding social obligations promised mystery, cabals, secrets to be imparted to the privileged few. The date suggested was not really convenient and Dalgliesh rearranged his diary with some reluctance while reflecting that one of the disadvantages of advancing age was an increasing disinclination for social engagements combined with an inability to summon the wit or energy to circumvent them. The friendship between them – he supposed the word was appropriate enough; they were certainly not mere acquaintances – was based on the use each occasionally made of the other. Since both acknowledged the fact, neither could see that it needed justification or excuse. Conrad, one of the most notorious and reliable gossips in London, had often been useful to him, notably in the Berowne case. On this occasion Dalgliesh would obviously be expected to confer the benefit, but the demand in whatever form it came would probably be more irritating than onerous, the food at the Cadaver was excellent and Ackroyd, although he could be facetious, was seldom dull.

Later he was to see all the horrors that followed as emanating from that perfectly ordinary luncheon, and would find himself thinking: if this were fiction and I were a novelist, that's where it would all begin.

The Cadaver Club is not among the most prestigious of London's private clubs but its coterie of members find it among the most convenient. Built in the 1800s, it was originally the house of a wealthy if not particularly successful barrister who, in 1892, bequeathed it, suitably endowed, to a private club formed some five years earlier which had regularly met in his drawing-room. The club was and remains exclusively masculine, the main qualification for membership being a professional interest in murder. Now, as then, it lists among the members a few retired senior police officers, practising and retired barristers, nearly all of the most distinguished professional and amateur criminologists, crime reporters, and a few eminent crime-novelists, all male and there on sufferance since the club takes the view that, where murder is concerned, fiction cannot compete with real life. The club had recently been in danger of moving from the category of eccentric to the dangerous one of fashionable, a risk which the committee had promptly countered by blackballing the next six applicants for admission.

The message was received. As one disgruntled applicant complained, to be blackballed by the Garrick is embarrassing, but to be blackballed by the Cadaver is ridiculous. The club kept itself small and, by its eccentric standards, select.

Crossing Tavistock Square, in the mellow September sunshine, Dalgliesh wondered how Ackroyd qualified as a member until he recalled the book his host had written five years earlier on three notorious murderers: Hawley Harvey Crippen, Norman Thorne and Patrick Mahon. Ackroyd had sent him a signed copy and Dalgliesh, dutifully reading it, had been surprised at the careful research and the even more careful writing. Ackroyd's thesis, not entirely original, had been that all three were innocent in the sense that none had intended to kill his victim, and Ackroyd had made a plausible, if not entirely convincing case, based on a detailed examination of the medical and forensic evidence. For Dalgliesh the main message of the book had been that men wishing to be acquitted of murder should avoid dismembering their victims, a practice for which British juries have long demonstrated their distaste.

They were to meet in the library for a sherry before luncheon and Ackroyd was already there ensconced in one of the leather high-backed chairs. He got to his feet with surprising agility for one of his size and came towards Dalgliesh with small, rather prancing steps, looking not a day older than when they had first met.

He said: 'It's good of you to make time, Adam. I realize how busy you are now. Special adviser to the Commissioner, member of the working party on regional crime squads and an occasional murder investigation to keep your hand in. You mustn't let them overwork you, dear boy. I'll ring for sherry. I thought of inviting you to my other club but you know how it is. Lunching there is a useful way of reminding people that you're still alive, but the members will come up and congratulate you on the fact. We'll be downstairs in the Snug.'

Ackroyd had married in late middle age, to the astonishment and consternation of his friends, and lived in connubial self-sufficiency in an agreeable Edwardian villa in St John's Wood where he and Nelly Ackroyd devoted themselves to their house and garden, their two Siamese cats and Ackroyd's largely imaginary ailments. He owned, edited and financed from a substantial private income *The Paternoster Review*, that iconoclastic mixture of literary articles, reviews and gossip, the last carefully researched, occasionally discreet, more often as malicious as it was accurate. Nelly, when not ministering to her husband's hypochondria, was an enthusiastic collector of 1920s and 1930s girls' school stories. The marriage was a success although Conrad's friends still had to remind themselves to ask after Nelly's health before inquiring about the cats.

The last time Dalgliesh had been in the library the visit had been professional and he had been in search of information. But then the case had been murder and he had been greeted by a different host. Little seemed to have changed. The room faced south over the square and this morning was warm with sunlight which, filtering through the fine white curtains, made the thin fire almost unnecessary. Originally the drawing-room, it now served both as sitting-room and library. The walls were lined with mahogany cases which held what was probably the most comprehensive private library of books on crime in London, including all the volumes of the *Notable British Trials* and *Famous Trials* series, books on medical jurisprudence, forensic pathology and policing and the club's few first editions of Conan Doyle, Poe, Le Fanu and Wilkie Collins, in a smaller case as if to demonstrate fiction's innate inferiority to reality. The large mahogany showcase was still in place, filled with articles collected or donated over the years; the prayer book with the signature, Constance Kent, on the flyleaf, the flintlock duelling pistol, supposedly used by the Reverend James Hackman for the murder of Margaret Wray, mistress of the Earl of Sandwich, a phial of white powder, allegedly arsenic, found in the possession of Major Herbert Armstrong. There was an addition since Dalgliesh's last visit. It lay curled, sinister as a lethal snake, in pride of place beneath a label stating that this was the rope with which Crippen had been hanged. Dalgliesh, turning to follow Ackroyd out of the library, mildly suggested that the public display of this distasteful object was barbaric, a protest which Ackroyd as mildly repudiated.

'A trifle morbid, perhaps, but barbaric is going a little far. After all, this isn't the Athenaeum. It probably does some of the older members good to be reminded of the natural end of their previous professional activities. Would you still be a detective if we hadn't abolished hanging?'

'I don't know. Abolition doesn't help with that particular moral dilemma as far as I'm concerned, since personally I would prefer death to twenty years in prison.'

'Not death by hanging?'

'No, not that.'

Hanging, for him, as he suspected for most people, had always held a particular horror. Despite the reports of Royal Commissions on capital punishment which claimed for it humanity, speed and the certainty of instantaneous death, it remained for him one of the ugliest forms of judicial execution encumbered with horrifying images as precisely lined as a pen drawing: mass victims in the wake of triumphant armies, the pathetic, half-demented victims of seventeenth-century justice, the muted drums of the quarterdecks of ships where the navy exacted its revenge and issued its warning, women convicted in the eighteenth century of infanticide, that ridiculous but sinister ritual of the small black square formally placed atop the judge's wig, the concealed but ordinary-looking door leading from the condemned cell to that last brief walk. It was good that they were all part of history. For a moment the Cadaver Club was a less agreeable place in which to lunch, its eccentricities more repugnant than amusing.

The Snug at the Cadaver Club is well named. It is a small basement room at the rear of the house with two windows and a french door opening on to a narrow paved courtyard bounded by a ten-foot ivied wall. The yard could comfortably accommodate three tables, but the members of the club are not addicted to dining outside, even in the occasional hot spell of an English summer, apparently regarding the habit as a foreign eccentricity incompatible with the proper appreciation of food or the privacy necessary to good talk. To dissuade any member who might be tempted to this indulgence, the courtyard is furnished with terracotta pots of various sizes planted with geraniums and ivy, and space further restricted by a huge stone copy of the Apollo Belvedere propped in the wall against the corner and rumoured to be the gift of an early member of the club whose wife had banished it from their suburban garden. The geraniums were still in full bloom and the bright pinks and reds glowed through the glass enhancing the immediate impression of welcoming domesticity. The room had obviously once been the kitchen and one wall was still fitted with the original iron grate, its bars and ovens polished now to ebony. The blackened beam above was hung with iron cooking instruments and a row of copper pans, battered but gleaming. An oak dresser ran the whole length of the opposite wall, serving as a receptacle for the display of the gifts and bequests of members which were deemed unsuitable for, or unworthy of, the library cabinet.

Dalgliesh remembered that the club had an unwritten law that no offering from a member, however inappropriate or bizarre, should be rejected and the dresser, like the whole room, bore witness to the idiosyncratic tastes and hobbies of the donors. Delicate Meissen plates were ranged in incongruous proximity to Victorian ribbon-decorated souvenirs bearing pictures of Brighton and Southend-on-Sea, a toby jug which looked like a fairground trophy stood between a Victorian Staffordshire flatback, obviously original, of Wesley preaching from a double-decker pulpit, and a fine Parian bust of the Duke of Wellington. An assortment of coronation mugs and early Staffordshire cups was suspended in precarious disorder from the hooks. Beside the door hung a painted glass picture of the burial of Princess Charlotte; above it a stuffed elk's head with an old Panama hat slung on its left horn gazed glassy-eyed with lugubrious disapproval at a large and lurid print of the Charge of the Light Brigade.

The present kitchen was somewhere close; Dalgliesh could hear small agreeable tinklings and from time to time the thud of the food lift descending from the first-floor dining-room. Only one of the four tables was set, the linen immaculate, and

Dalgliesh and Ackroyd seated themselves beside the window.

The menu and wine list were already to the right of Ackroyd's place. Taking them up, he said: 'The Plants have retired, but we've got the Jacksons now, and I'm not sure that Mrs Jackson's cooking isn't even better. We were lucky to get them. She and her husband used to run a private nursing home but they got tired of the country and wanted to return to London. They don't need to work but I think the job suits them. They've kept on with the policy of having only one main dish a day at luncheon and dinner. Very wise. Today, white bean and tuna fish salad followed by rack of lamb with fresh vegetables and a green salad. Then lemon tart and cheese to follow. The vegetables will be fresh. We still get all the vegetables and eggs from young Plant's smallholding. Do you want to see the wine list? Have you a preference?'

'I'll leave that to you.'

Ackroyd cogitated aloud while Dalgliesh, who loved wine but disliked talking about it, let his gaze range appreciatively over the muddle of a room which despite, perhaps because of, its air of eccentric but organized chaos was surprisingly restful. The discordant objects, not carefully placed for effect, had through time achieved a rightness of place. After a lengthy discussion on the merits of the wine list in which Ackroyd apparently expected no contribution from his guest, he fixed on a chardonnay. Mrs Jackson, appearing as if in response to some secret signal, brought with her the smell of hot rolls and an air of bustling confidence.

'Very nice to meet you, Commander. You've got the Snug to yourself this morning, Mr Ackroyd. Mr Jackson will be seeing to the wine.'

After the first course had been served, Dalgliesh said: 'Why is Mrs Jackson dressed as a nurse?'

'Because she is one, I suppose. She used to be a matron. She's a midwife too, I believe, but we've no call for that here.'

Not surprisingly, thought Dalgliesh, since the club didn't admit women. He said: 'Isn't that goffered cap with streamers going a bit far?'

'Oh, do you think so? I suppose we've got used to it. I doubt if the members would feel at home if Mrs Jackson stopped wearing it now.'

Ackroyd wasted no time in coming to the purpose of the meeting. As soon as they were finally alone he said: 'Lord Stilgoe had a word with me last week in Brooks's. He's my wife's uncle, incidentally. Do you know him?'

'No. I thought he was dead.'

'I can't think how you got that idea.' He prodded at his bean salad irritably and Dalgliesh remembered that he resented any suggestion that someone he knew personally could actually die, and certainly not without the prior knowledge of himself. 'He isn't even as old as he looks, not eighty yet. He's remarkably spry for his age. Actually he's publishing his memoirs. The Peverell Press are bringing them out next spring. That's what he wanted to see me about. Something rather worrying has happened. At least his wife finds it worrying. She thinks he's had a direct threat of murder.'

'And has he?'

'Well, he's received this.'

He took some time in taking the small oblong of paper from his wallet and passing it over to Dalgliesh. The words had been accurately typed on a word processor and the message was unsigned.

'Do you really think it wise to publish with Peverell Press? Remember Marcus Seabright, Joan Petrie and now Sonia Clements. Two authors and your own editor dead in less than twelve months. Do you want to be number four?'

Dalgliesh said: 'More mischievous than threatening, I should have thought, and the malice directed against the Press rather than Stilgoe. There's no doubt that Sonia Clements' death was suicide. She left a note for the coroner and wrote to her sister telling her that she intended to kill herself. I don't recall anything about the first two deaths.'

'Oh, they're straightforward enough, I should have thought. Seabright was over eighty and had a bad heart. He died from an attack of gastroenteritis which brought on a heart attack. Anyway, he was no loss to Peverell Press. He hadn't produced a novel for ten years. Joan Petrie killed herself driving to her country cottage. Accidental death. Petrie had two passions, whisky and fast cars. The only surprise is that she killed herself before she killed someone else. Obviously the poison pen dragged up these two deaths as makeweights. But Dorothy Stilgoe is superstitious. She takes the view, why publish with Peverell when there are other publishers?'

'And who is actually in charge now?'

'Oh Gerard Etienne. Very much so. The last chairman and managing director, old Henry Peverell, died in early January and left his shares in the business in equal parts to his daughter Frances and to Gerard. His original partner, Jean-Philippe Etienne, had retired about a year previously, and not before time. His shares also went to Gerard. The two older men ran the firm as if it was their private hobby. Old Peverell always took the view that a gentleman inherited money, he didn't earn it. Jean-Philippe Etienne hadn't taken an active part in the firm for years. His moment of glory, of course, was in the last war where he was a hero of the Resistance in Vichy France, but I don't think he's done anything memorable since. Gerard was waiting in the wings, the crown prince. And now he's well on stage and we're likely to see action if not melodrama.'

'Does Gabriel Dauntsey still run the poetry list?'

'I'm surprised you need to ask, Adam. You mustn't let your passion for catching murderers put you out of touch with real life. Yes, he's still there. He hasn't written a poem himself for over twenty years. Dauntsey's an anthology poet. The best is so good that it keeps reappearing, but I imagine most readers think he's dead. He was a bomber pilot in the last war so he must be well over seventy. It's time he retired. The poetry list at Peverell Press is about all he does nowadays. The other three partners are Gerard's sister Claudia Etienne, James de Witt, who's been with the firm since he left Oxford, and Frances Peverell, the last of the Peverells. But it's Gerard who runs the firm.'

'What is he planning, do you know?'

'Rumour has it that he wants to sell Innocent House and move to Docklands. That won't please Frances Peverell. The Peverells have always had an obsession about Innocent House. It belongs to the partnership now, not to the family, but any Peverell thinks of it as the family home. He's already made other changes, some staff sacked, including Sonia Clements. He's right, of course. The firm has got to be dragged into the twentieth century or go under, but he's certainly made enemies. It's significant that they had no trouble at the Press until Gerard took over. That coincidence hasn't escaped Stilgoe, although his wife is still convinced that the malice is directed against her husband personally, not the firm, and against his memoirs in particular.'

'Will Peverell lose much if the book is withdrawn?'

'Not a great deal, I imagine. Of course they'll hype the memoirs as if their disclosures could bring down the Government, discredit the Opposition and end parliamentary democracy as we know it, but I imagine that, like most political memoirs, they'll promise more than they deliver. But I don't see how it can be withdrawn. The book is in production, they won't let it go without a struggle, and Stilgoe won't want to break the contract if it means publicly explaining why. What Dorothy Stilgoe is asking is, was Sonia Clements' death really suicide and did someone interfere with Petrie's Jag? I think she's satisfied enough that old Seabright died from natural causes.'

'So what am I expected to do?'

'There must have been inquests in the last two cases and presumably the police carried out an investigation. Your people could take a look at the papers, have a word with the officers concerned, that sort of thing. Then, if Dorothy could be assured that a senior Metropolitan detective has looked at all the evidence and is satisfied, she might give her husband, and Peverell Press, some peace.'

Dalgliesh said: 'That might serve to satisfy her that Sonia Clements' death was suicide. It will hardly content her if she's superstitious, and I don't see what will. The essence of superstition is that it isn't amenable to reason. She'll probably take the view that an unlucky publisher is as bad as a murderous one. I suppose she isn't seriously suggesting that someone at Peverell Press put an unidentifiable poison in Sonia Clements' wine?'

'No, I don't think she's going as far as that.'

'Just as well or her husband will have his profits eaten up by a libel action. I'm surprised he didn't go straight to the Commissioner or to me direct.'

'Are you? I'm not sure. It would have looked – well, shall we say a little timid, a trifle over-concerned. Besides he doesn't know you, I do. I can understand why he spoke to me first. And of course, one can hardly see him calling in at the local nick, joining the queue of lost-dog owners, assaulted wives and aggrieved motorists and explaining his dilemma to the duty sergeant. Frankly I don't think he believed it would be taken seriously. His view is that, having regard to his wife's concern and that anonymous note, he's justified in asking the police to take a look at what is happening at the Peverell Press.'

The lamb had arrived, pink and succulent and tender enough to be eaten with a spoon. In the few minutes of silence which Ackroyd thought a necessary tribute to a perfectly cooked meal, Dalgliesh recalled the first time he had seen Innocent House.

His father had taken him to London for his eighth birthday treat; they were to spend two whole days sight-seeing and stay overnight with a friend, who was a parish priest in Kensington, and his wife. He could remember lying in bed the night before, fitfully sleeping and almost sick with excitement, the cavernous immensity and clamour of the old Liverpool Street Station, his terror of losing his father, of being caught up and swept along with the great army of grey-faced marching people. In the two days in which his father had intended to combine pleasure with education – to his scholarly mind the two were indistinguishable – they had perhaps inevitably tried to do too much.

The visit had been overwhelming for an eight-year-old, leaving a confused memory of churches and galleries, restaurants and unfamiliar food, of floodlit towers and the dancing reflection of light on the black creased surface of the water, of sleek, prancing horses and silver helmets, of the glamour and terror of history made manifest in brick and stone. But London had laid on him her spell which no adult experience, no exploration of other great cities had been able to break.

It was on the second day that they had visited Westminster Abbey and later taken a river steamer from Charing Cross pier to Greenwich and he had first seen Innocent House, glittering in the morning sun, seeming to rise like a golden mirage from the shimmering water. He had gazed at it in wonder. His father had explained that the name was derived from Innocent Walk which ran behind the house, at the end of which had once stood an early eighteenth-century magistrates' court. Defendants taken into custody after their first hearing were removed to the Fleet prison; the more fortunate walked down the cobbled lane to freedom. He had started to tell his son something of the house's architectural history, but his voice had been overpowered by the tour-guide's booming commentary, loud enough to be heard by every boat on the river.

'And here, coming up on our left, ladies and gentlemen, is one of the most interesting buildings on the Thames: Innocent House, built in 1830 for Sir Francis

Peverell, a noted publisher of the day. Sir Francis had visited Venice and had been very impressed by the Ca' d'Oro, the Golden House on the Grand Canal. Those of you who have had holidays in Venice have probably seen it. So he hit on the idea of building his own golden house on the Thames. Pity he couldn't import Venetian weather.' He paused briefly for the expected laughter. 'Today it is the headquarters of a publishing firm, the Peverell Press, so it's still in the family. There's an interesting story about Innocent House. Apparently Sir Francis was so absorbed by it that he neglected his young wife whose money had helped him to build it, and she threw herself from the top balcony and was instantly killed. The legend has it that you can still see the stain of her blood on the marble which can't be cleaned away. It's said that Sir Francis went mad with remorse in his old age and used to go out alone at night trying to get rid of that tell-tale spot. It's his ghost that people claim to see, still scrubbing away at the stain. There are some watermen who don't like sailing too close to Innocent House after dark.'

All eyes on deck had been docilely turned to the house but now, intrigued by this story of blood, the passengers moved to hang over the rail; voices murmured and heads craned as if the legendary stain might still be visible. Eight-year-old Adam's over-vivid imagination had pictured a white-clad woman, blonde hair flying, flinging herself from the balcony like some demented storybook heroine, had heard the final thud and seen the trickle of blood creeping and starting across the marble to drip into the Thames. For years afterwards the house had continued to fascinate him with a potent amalgam of beauty and terror.

The tour-guide had been inaccurate about one fact; it was possible that the suicide story had also been embellished or untrue. He knew now that Sir Francis had been enchanted, not by the Ca' d'Oro which, despite the intricacies of its fine tracings and carvings, he had found, or so he had written to his architect, too asymmetrical for his taste, but by the Palace of Doge Francesco Foscari, and it was the Ca' Foscari which his architect had been instructed to build for him on this cold, tidal river. It should have looked incongruous, a folly, unmistakably Venetian and Venetian of the mid-fifteenth century. And yet it looked as if no other city, no other site would have been right for it. Dalgliesh still found it difficult to understand why it should be so successful, this unashamed borrowing from another age, another country, a softer, warmer air. The proportions had been changed and surely that alone should have rendered Sir Francis's dream an impracticable presumption, but the reduction in scale had been brilliantly carried out and the dignity of the original somehow maintained. There were six great central window arches instead of eight behind the finely carved balconies of the first and second floors, but the marble columns with their decorated pinnules were almost exact copies of the Venetian palace and the central arcades here, as there, were balanced by tall single windows, giving the façade its unity and grace. The great curved door fronted a marble patio leading to a landing-stage and a flight of steps to the river. On either side of the house two brick-built Regency town houses with small balconies, presumably built to house coachmen or other servants, stood like humble sentries of the central magnificence. He had seen it from the river many times since that eighth-birthday celebration but had never been inside. He recalled having read that there was a fine Matthew Cotes Wyatt ceiling in the central hall and rather wished he could see it. It would be a pity if Innocent House fell into the hands of philistines.

He asked: 'And what exactly has been going on at Peverell Press? What's worrying Lord Stilgoe apart from his poison-pen letter?'

'So you've heard the rumours. Difficult to tell. They're being rather cagey about it and I don't blame them. But one or two little incidents have become common knowledge. Not so little either. The most serious happened just before Easter when they lost the illustrations for Gregory Maybrick's book on the Guy Fawkes conspiracy. Popular history, no doubt, but Maybrick knows his period. They expected to do rather well with it. He'd managed to lay his hands on some interesting contemporary plates, never before published, as well as other written records, and the whole lot were lost. They were on loan from the various owners and he'd more or less guaranteed their safety.'

'Lost? Mislaid? Destroyed?'

'The story is that he delivered them by hand to James de Witt who was editing the book. He's their senior editor and normally responsible for fiction but old Peverell who edited their non-fiction had died about three months earlier and I suppose they either hadn't had time to find a suitable replacement or wanted to save money. Like most houses they're laying off rather than taking on. The rumour is that they can't keep afloat much longer. Not surprising with that Venetian palace to maintain. Anyway, the illustrations were handed over to de Witt in his office and he locked them in his cupboard while Maybrick watched.'

'Not in a safe?'

'My dear boy, we're talking about a publishing house not Cartier's. Knowing Peverells, I'm only surprised that de Witt bothered to lock the cupboard.'

'Was his the only key?'

'Really, Adam, you're not detecting now. Actually it was. He kept it in a battered old tobacco tin in his left-hand drawer.'

Where else? thought Dalgliesh. He said: 'Where any member of the staff or any unaccompanied visitor could lay hands on it.'

'Well, someone obviously did. James didn't need to go to the cupboard for a couple of days. The illustrations were due to be delivered personally to the art department the following week. You know that Peverells have put out their artwork to an independent firm?'

'No, I didn't know.'

'More economical, I suppose. It's the same firm that's been doing the jackets for the last five years. Rather well, actually. Peverells have never let their standards slip on book production and design. You can always tell a Peverell book just by handling it. Until now, of course. Gerard Etienne may change that too. Anyway, when de Witt looked for the envelope it had disappeared. Huge fuss, of course. Everyone questioned. Frantic searches. General panic. In the end they had to confess to Maybrick and the owners. You can imagine how they took the news.'

'Did the stuff ever come to light?'

'Not until too late. There were doubts whether Maybrick would want to publish at all but the book was in the catalogue and it was decided to go ahead with alternative illustrations and some necessary changes to the text. A week after they'd finished printing, the envelope and its contents mysteriously reappeared. De Witt found it in his cupboard exactly where he had placed it.'

'Which suggests that the thief had some respect for scholarship and had never intended to destroy the papers.'

'It suggests a number of possibilities, spite against Maybrick, spite against the Press, spite against de Witt, or a somewhat warped sense of humour.'

'Peverells didn't report the theft to the police?'

'No, Adam, they didn't place their confidence in our wonderful boys in blue. I don't want to be unkind but the police haven't an impressive clear-up rate when it comes to domestic burglary. The partners took the view that they stood just as good a chance of success and would cause less upset to staff if they undertook their own inquiry.'

'By whom? Were any of them free of suspicion?'

'That, of course, is the difficulty. They weren't then and they aren't now. I imagine that Etienne adopted the Head Beak's strategy. You know, 'If the boy who's responsible will come to my study after prep in confidence and return the documents no more will be heard of the matter.' It never worked at school. I don't suppose it was more successful at Peverells. It was obviously an inside job, and it isn't as if they employ a large staff, only about twenty-five people in addition to the five partners. Most of them are old faithfuls, of course, and the story is that the few who aren't have alibis.'

'So it's still a mystery.'

'And so is the second incident. The second serious incident – there have probably been minor mischiefs which they've managed to keep quiet about. This one concerns Stilgoe so it's just as well that so far they've managed to keep it from him and it hasn't become public property. The old boy really would have some-thing to feed his paranoia. Apparently when the page proofs had been read and a number of alterations agreed with Stilgoe they were packaged and left overnight under the counter in the reception office where they were due to be collected next morning. Someone opened the package and tampered with them, changed a number of the names, altered punctuation, deleted a couple of sentences. Fortunately the printer who received them was intelligent and thought some of the changes odd, so he telephoned to check. The partners have managed, God knows how, to keep this contretemps secret from most of the staff at Innocent House and, of course, from Stilgoe. It would have been extremely damaging to the firm if it had got out. I understand all parcels and papers are locked up overnight now and no doubt they've tightened security in other ways.'

Dalgliesh wondered whether the perpetrator had from the first intended the alterations to be discovered. They seemed to have been made with very little attempt to deceive. It surely wouldn't have been difficult to alter the page proofs in a way which would seriously damage the book without arousing the suspicions of the printer. It was odd, too, that the poison pen hadn't mentioned the alterations to Stilgoe's proofs. Either he or she hadn't known, which would absolve the five partners, or the poison pen had wanted to frighten Stilgoe but not to provide evidence which would justify him in withdrawing the book. It was an interesting little mystery but not one on which he proposed to waste the time of a senior police officer.

Nothing more was said about the Peverell Press until they were taking their coffee in the library. Ackroyd leaned forward and asked a little anxiously, 'Can I tell Lord Stilgoe that you'll try to reassure his wife?'

'I'm sorry, Conrad, but no. I'll get him a note to say that the police have no cause to suspect foul play in any of the cases which concern him. I doubt whether it will do much good if his wife is superstitious, but that is her misfortune and his problem.'

'And the other trouble at Innocent House?'

'If Gerard Etienne believes that the law is being broken and wants the police to investigate he must get in touch with his local station.'

'Just like anybody else?'

'Precisely.'

'You wouldn't be prepared to go to Innocent House and have an informal word with him?'

'No, Conrad. Not even for a sight of the Wyatt ceiling.'

But it was to be murder, not suicide, that brought Dalgliesh and his team to Innocent House.

POCKET PENGUINS

POCKET PENGUINS